Screw Loose

by

Alison Prince

Alison Prince, writer of over 30 children's books and winner of the Guardian Children's Fiction Award, is also the biographer of Kenneth Grahame and Hans Christian Andersen. She lives on the Isle of Arran with two cats and a dog, and won the *Literary Review* Grand Poetry Prize in 1997.

Illustrated by Judith Lawton

To all those who have ever wished things were different

Barrington Stoke has enchanted and inspired generations with his stories. He would go from village to village, arriving at twilight and carrying a lantern to light his way and signal his arrival. In the village meeting place he set down his lantern and placed five stones in a circle. Barrington Stoke stood at the front of the circle in the light of his lantern. In the flickering light the children sat entranced while he told the tale. And then another. And then another, until they were tired and ready for sleep. But Barrington Stoke's imagination was never exhausted - he moved on to the next day, the next village, the next story.

First published in Great Britain by Barrington Stoke Ltd
10 Belford Terrace, Edinburgh, EH4 3DQ
Copyright © 1998 Alison Prince
Illustrations © 1998 Judith Lawton
The moral right of the author has been asserted in accordance
with the Copyright, Designs and Patents Act 1988
ISBN 1-902260-01-5
Printed by BPC Ltd, Aberdeen

Contents

Chapter One   1

Chapter Two   11

Chapter Three   19

Chapter Four   29

Chapter Five   51

Chapter One

Roddy Watt found the screwdriver by the school gate. It was lying on the tarmac. It was a short, strong screwdriver with a stubby handle, just the right size to fit into his pocket.

He unscrewed a coat-hook in the cloakroom with no bother at all, and smiled. Then he put the screwdriver back in his pocket and went upstairs for registration. Nobody had seen him, because he was late, as usual.

'Roderick Watt, you are late, as usual,' said his class teacher, Mrs Bigg.

'That's right, Miss,' agreed Roddy. 'Sorry.'

Mrs Bigg sighed and asked, 'Why are you always late?'

'Dunno,' said Roddy.

Wasn't it obvious? Nobody in their right mind would want to come into this place with its stupid baby-blue paint and its posters about drug-taking. Who would want to spend a day being bored?

It was better to hang about a bit on the way and go into the shop with the *Daily Record* posters outside before he got on the bus. He often took some time choosing which crisps to buy and what kind of chewing gum. Still, he had the screwdriver now. That would make things more interesting.

'I might be early tomorrow,' he said.

'Oh, good,' said Mrs Bigg.

Roddy was in school the next day before anyone else. He unscrewed a notice on the Head's door, a window-catch or two and the hinges to the door of the boys' toilet. He slackened off the brackets that held up the shelves in his classroom. The door opened as he was dealing with a couple of tables. Biff came in with her usual armful of magazines.

'Hi,' she said. 'Why are you so early?'

'Just thought I'd have a change,' said Roddy. 'Why are *you* early?'

'My Mum does an early-morning job at the hospital,' Biff said. 'Cleaning. So I go with her before school. That's where I get the magazines. People give loads of them to the hospital, and the nurse chucks out the old ones. New ones, too, if they're sexy or about motorbikes and things.'

She dumped her armful on the nearest table, which lurched and fell sideways.

'This place makes you sick,' she said. 'Why don't they spend some money on it.'

Roddy tried not to look guilty.

'The leg's come unscrewed,' he said as he picked the table up. He fished the screwdriver out of his pocket and hoped Biff would not notice that the screws were in there as well. But she did, of course.

'So that's why you were so early,' she said. 'Hey, was it you who undid the KNOCK and WAIT notice off Mr Pimm's door? I saw it lying on the floor.'

'Could have been,' said Roddy and shrugged.

Biff laughed.

'Great!' she said. 'Wait till I tell Debbie and Sheena!'

'Give me a break,' said Roddy. 'Don't go telling everyone. If the jannie gets to know, I'm dead.'

'What's a jannie?' asked a voice from the door.

Roddy and Biff turned to see Tim Tomkins standing there, with his floppy fair hair falling over one eye. Tim had just come to Glasgow from London, and didn't know anything about anything.

'It's the janitor,' Biff told him. 'He looks after the building, does the boilers and that. Or sometimes the janitor's a she.'

'Is that the guy called Mr Rundle?' asked Tim. 'Wears a navy uniform, got that little office near the bogs?'

'That's right,' said Roddy.

'So what mustn't he get to know?' Tim asked.

'Nothing,' said Biff and Roddy together.

Tim nodded a couple of times. Then he wandered over to his place and sat down. He looked so miserable that after a few minutes they told him about the screwdriver. But Roddy threatened fatal damage to his Game Boy if he let on.

Chapter Two

The usual crowd was milling round the chip van at lunch break. Roddy went into the boys' toilet to do some more unscrewing. He found Mr Rundle busy replacing the door hinges.

'You're supposed to be outside,' said Mr Rundle.

'I just needed a pee,' said Roddy.

'On you go, then.'

Roddy didn't need a pee at all, and found it difficult to produce much with Mr Rundle watching him.

'What's the matter with the door?' Roddy asked, in an innocent voice.

'We're having an attack of deconstruction,' said Mr Rundle.

'What's that?'

Mr Rundle sighed.

'Don't they teach you anything these days? Construction is putting things together, right? Deconstruction is taking them apart. Somebody around here has been taking things apart.'

'Go on,' said Roddy.

Mr Rundle fixed him with an accusing eye.

'And what's more, one of my screwdrivers is missing. Short one, with a stubby handle. You've not seen it, have you?'

'No!' Roddy's voice sounded a bit squeaky, even to himself.

'I'll be wanting it returned,' said Mr Rundle.

And as Roddy went out, trying to look casual, he felt Mr Rundle's gaze drilling into his back.

After that, unscrewing things became a risky game, although it was fun. Roddy knew he was giving Mr Rundle a lot of work, but it was so great to have a real interest in school that he couldn't stop.

He watched carefully to make sure nobody was about before loosening desk legs and notice boards and the framed portrait of some old bird who had been the first Head Teacher of the school.

Roddy was extra proud of this, because the portrait hung just outside the office of the present Head, Mr Pimm. He was a thin, stiff man who did not understand jokes. He wore a dark blue suit with pin stripes, and Roddy thought he looked just like a Bic Biro.

Mr Pimm seemed to get even thinner as the unscrewing epidemic went on. He kept bleating in Assembly about the tide of vandalism engulfing the school. He would nervously snatch his glasses off and on and run his fingers through what was left of his hair.

Roddy was glad the Head did not have the sense to offer a reward for information, because the secret was well and truly out now. Somebody would have cracked then and there if the money had been right. Dave Boyle's gang, who did most of the graffiti and general destruction, were really annoyed that they had not thought of it first.

Stupid Joe Picken had a go at it, but he used a huge great screwdriver that fell out of his sports bag in Media Studies. He got suspended, of course, but he didn't mind, because it gave him more time for his shop-lifting. And Mr Pimm was even more upset when the unscrewing still did not stop.

Mr Pimm called in the Crime Prevention Officer (CPO for short) to talk to the school at Assembly. The CPO looked a bit like a social

worker, Roddy thought, with a sports jacket over his police trousers. He went on about how awful it was to enter a life of crime.

Davey Boyle's gang were so interested that they hardly made any noise. But when Mr Pimm stepped to the lectern to thank the CPO, the top of it fell off. It hit him on the big toe. He stood there on one foot, trying not to hop, while everyone fell off their chairs laughing. It was one of Roddy's absolute triumphs, and even the Crime Prevention Officer was grinning, though he blew his nose to try and hide it.

Chapter Three

The next morning, Mr Rundle was waiting in a van outside the entry to Roddy's flat.

'You're wanted,' he said through the van's open window. 'Get in.'

'Wanted?' Roddy's heart thumped.

So the game was up. If you were wanted, it had to mean the police.

'Where are we going?' he asked, trying to sound calm.

'School, of course. But they asked me to have a word with you first.'

Mr Rundle glanced over his shoulder, put the van in gear and set off down the road.

'You see, Mr Pimm's been taken ill.'

'What sort of ill?'

'Mental. His wife phoned this morning to say he was under the table, barking. You've to take over.'

Roddy frowned.

'What d'you mean, take over?'

'What I say. You're to be the new Head. They had the good sense to come to me, I'm glad to say. *Mr Rundle,* they said, *if there's one person in a school who knows the score, it's the jannie.* Right enough, of course. So I suggested you.'

This could not be real, Roddy thought. Why him, why? But at the back of his mind, he knew why.

Mr Rundle stopped at traffic lights and turned to look at him.

'I know you, son,' he said. 'Like they say, you don't have to be mad to be a Head, but it helps. And you've a bit of a screw loose, as you might say. Right?'

Roddy felt his face redden. Mr Rundle held out his hand and said,

'You'd best give me that screwdriver before we get any further. Could be tricky if you got caught with it. You being the Head and all.'

Roddy fished in his pocket for the short, stubby screwdriver. He would miss it.

'Thanks,' said Mr Rundle, dropping it into his own pocket. 'I've missed that.'

Roddy nodded. He understood how he felt.

'Sorry,' he said.

'That's all right.' The jannie drove on.

As they neared the school, Roddy said, 'I'm not dreaming, am I?'

'You could be,' said Mr Rundle. 'All I know is, I'm not.'

Panic hit Roddy as if he had stepped out of an aeroplane at two thousand feet.

'I can't do this,' he said desperately. 'Run the school? You must be joking, aren't you? Tell me you are.'

'No,' said Mr Rundle. 'I'm not joking. It's a stupid idea, I'll give you that, and I told them so, but that's what they want. Try it out, they said. When all the usual things fail, experiment with something new.'

'But what'll I *do*?' shrieked Roddy.

'Anything you like. You're not allowed to sack the teachers, though. Not yet. You can do that later if you like, but it takes time to cook up the excuses.'

Roddy nodded, thinking fast.

'Does everyone know it's me in charge?'

'Your name's on the office door,' said Mr Rundle. 'And the staff have been told. You might find Mr Harris helpful.'

He swung into the car-park behind the boiler room and switched the engine off.

Chapter Four

Roddy saw the neat, new name-plate on the door at the Head's office, MR RODERICK WATT, HEADMASTER.

'I'll be calling you Mr Watt in future,' Mr Rundle said, as he ushered him in. 'At least, in front of the kids.'

Roddy crossed to the desk with a leather top and sat down behind it. He felt very small.

'What'll I do?' he asked again and knew the question sounded pathetic.

'Have a meeting,' advised Mr Rundle. 'That's what they all do when in doubt. If you want to talk to the school, the button beside the mike on your desk is the PA. Public Address System,' he added, as Roddy looked blank. 'Best of luck.'

And he went out, shutting the door behind him.

Roddy spun about in the big office chair. He found that it would spin right round if he gave himself a good push off, and he did that a couple of times. Then he became aware of the noise which drifted up through the window. The school was outside, waiting for the bell that would ring in a couple of minutes.

Biff would be in the classroom already, getting her magazines organised for a day's reading. Tim too, probably, because he thought Biff was wonderful. And Dave Boyle's lot might be absolutely anywhere.

Roddy's tummy lurched uneasily as he thought about Dave Boyle. The bell rang, and he heard the hubbub grow louder as people poured into the building. He wished he was one of them, instead of being stuck here on his own.

A meeting, yes, that was the thing. He needed Biff in here. She was sensible, even if her spiky hair did look a bit funny. He needed one or two of the others as well. He pressed the button beside the microphone and said,

'Hello?'

His voice echoed back from the corridor outside.

For a moment, he panicked. What was Biff's real name? He must do this properly. He tried again.

'Will Barbara Irene Ferris please come to the Headmaster's office at once,' he said. 'And Tim Tomkins.'

Then he added, 'Biff can bring some friends if she likes. And Dave Boyle and his lot had better come too.'

But then there would be too many trouble-makers, so he said,

'In fact, anyone from Mrs Bigg's class can come if they're interested.'

The noise seemed to get more instead of less, and Roddy realised that none of the other classes knew what they were supposed to do. He pressed the button once more.

'Quiet!' he commanded. 'And listen.'

After a moment, he went on.

'Stay in your own classrooms for the first two periods. Discuss how you would like the school to be run, and write down some sensible notes. Use someone with decent handwriting. I don't want any scribbles from teachers. Bring the notes to my office at interval time, and I'll tell you then what to do next. Thank you.'

Biff was the first to come tumbling in through the office door.
She was followed by Dave Boyle who was doubled up. He was cursing loudly that she had kicked him somewhere painful.

'Shut up and sit down,' Roddy said bravely.

Dave stared at him.

'Who're you telling to -'

'SIT DOWN!' Roddy bellowed. 'We can't muck about, there are things to do.'

Dave grabbed one of the few chairs. He turned it the wrong way round and sat astride it, leaning his arms on the back.

'Go on, then, big man,' he sneered. 'While we let you.'

His gang grinned and nodded.

The whole of Mrs Bigg's class was piling into the room. At first it was bedlam, everyone talking at once and offering ideas.

Roddy found a notepad and scribbled hard, trying to get it all down. Debbie wanted to know why they should not eat in class, and Stewart said school should start at eleven and end at two, with an hour for lunch. Mike wanted to learn Greek.

A lot of people said teachers must not be sarcastic. Jenny said she would never get to University because you couldn't learn anything when people mucked about all the time. A lot of people agreed, but Dave Boyle's lot shouted them down. Danny didn't see why he had been banned from computing just because he had hacked into the school system.

He had used the sports allowance to bet on his Dad's greyhound. He had replaced the money when it won, hadn't he? Plus a share of the profit - they ought to be grateful.

Everyone was fed up about not being able to sack the teachers but Sheena said,

'Mrs Bigg's all right. She's strict, but you can see she likes us, really.'

'Mr Crawley should go,' said Stewart. 'My Mum says he doesn't correct half my spelling mistakes. How are you to know when it's wrong? No point in bothering.'

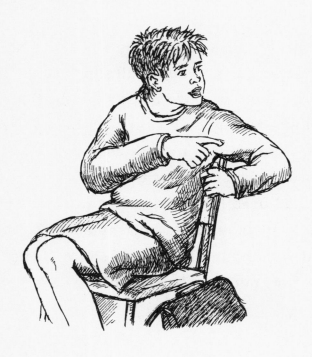

Dave's lot shouted and laughed so much that Roddy couldn't hear half of what people said, and at last Biff yelled,

'Look, SHUT UP!'

Then she said to Roddy,

'The worst of the problem is THEM, the trouble-makers. They ruin everything. Lessons are dead boring because the teachers spend their whole time trying to cope with them. We ought to chuck them out.'

'You can't, you stupid cow,' said Dave. 'It's the law. Think I'd be here two minutes if I didn't have to be?'

Uproar broke out again.

'LISTEN!' roared Roddy. When they were quieter he went on. 'What if we take Mr Harris off all other classes and put him in permanent charge of the trouble-makers?'

'Brilliant,' said Biff, amid shouts of protest.

'Harris is a monster,' yelled Kevin, but a boy called Peter shook his head.

'He's tough, but he's fair,' he said. 'When it was snowing last year and I got my jacket stolen, he lent me one he had in the back of his car.'

At that moment, Mr Rundle put his head round the door. He looked at Roddy Watt and said,

'All right, Mr Watt? Anything I can do?'

'Can I hold your hand, Mr Watt?' mocked Dave. 'Can I wipe your bum, Mr Watt?'

'There is something you can do,' Roddy said to Mr Rundle. 'We've decided to hand some of these people over to Mr Harris, full-time. So could you take them down to Mr Harris's room and give him this note?'

He scribbled busily.

'Tell him the class he's got now can come up here - I'll look after them until we can get things sorted out.'

'Right,' said Mr Rundle. 'I take it that'll be Dave Boyle and his lot?'

He glanced across the room and added, 'I'll also take that boy who's scribbling on the telephone directory, and those two girls shouting out of the window. Over here by the door, please.'

Somehow there was no arguing with Mr Rundle.

'Wow!' said Biff when the door closed. 'Isn't it quiet!'

'It's going to stay that way,' said Roddy.

He worked harder for the rest of the day than he had ever done in his life. Biff and the others wanted big changes. They wanted a 'self-service' timetable which let everyone choose from the lessons on offer. They also wanted help for Mr Harris in running his Sin Bin.

They asked for an agreement that anyone seriously mucking about in any other class would be sent to Mr Harris at once. And there would be a new deal with the staff, promising no chewing gum in class and no cheek, in exchange for prompt marking of work and a let-up on the sarcastic remarks.

Roddy struggled to write all this down in some sort of form that made sense. He didn't know if it would work or not. But at least it was worth a try.

At lunch-break, he was too busy reorganising Mr Harris's class to go down to the canteen or out to the chip-van. A pile of notes arrived from all the classes. His secretary came in and said she would type them out for him. She said he needed a break for a coffee and a sandwich.

'You'll have to learn to take it easy,' she told him, 'or you'll end up like poor Mr Pimm.'

Roddy was late home because he had called a meeting with the staff to explain the new arrangements. Some of them had been really awkward and argued a lot. He staggered in through the door and collapsed in a chair.

'What have you been up to?' his mother asked.

Roddy explained. His mother smiled and said it must be some sort of project. She and Roddy's father were both teachers themselves, so they tended to talk a lot about things like projects. Roddy was too tired to argue.

He just about managed to eat his tea before going upstairs to bed. In the bathroom, he was amazed to see the face gazing back at him from the mirror looking so old and tired.

Chapter Five

Next morning, Mr Rundle was not waiting outside in the van. Roddy got the early bus to school and made his way wearily to the office.

'And where are you going?' asked Mr Rundle, appearing behind him.

'Into the office. I mean -'

'No, you're not, son. Not unless you've been sent for.'

'But -'

Roddy looked at the name-plate on the door, MR RODERICK WATT, HEADMASTER.

'Yesterday, I -'

'Yesterday, we had a new Head. Same name as you.' Mr Rundle agreed. 'He's still here today. You wouldn't know, of course, since you took the day off. Bunking off school, were you?'

'No!' said Roddy indignantly. 'You know I wasn't. I was here. I was working really hard.'

Mr Rundle glanced up and down the empty corridor. Then he said quietly,

'We understand each other, son, don't we? Things will be different from now, you'll see. Now, away you go - and don't worry.'

Then he knocked, opened the office door and went in, closing it behind him.

Roddy caught a brief glimpse of the new Head who was sitting in the swivel chair behind the desk. His face looked old and tired, just as Roddy's face had done when he saw it in the mirror last night.

Roddy turned away, his mind reeling. Biff was coming through the door.

'Hi!' she said. 'Where were you yesterday? We've got this new Head. He's terrific. He's changing everything. And he's got the same name as you!'

'I know,' said Roddy.

'Do you?' She seemed surprised. 'Oh, OK then, I won't bother telling you.'

Then she thought of something.

'You'd better stop the unscrewing, or you'll end up with Dave Boyle and that lot in

Mr Harris's room. This Mr Watt's a lot tougher than old Pimm was. He's nice, though. We all like him.'

'I'm glad,' said Roddy.

He went down the corridor to the cloakroom. He pulled off his jacket, not sure if he was disappointed or relieved. What on earth had happened yesterday? Had he been dreaming? Who was the man in the office who shared his name?

It was crazy to think that there were two Roderick Watts. Could they have been the same person, just for one day?

The door of Mr Rundle's office stood open, as if on purpose. Roddy stopped and looked in. The short, stubby screwdriver was lying on the table in a clear space of its own.

A creepy feeling came over Roddy. He remembered when Mr Rundle had reached out for it in the van.

Mr Rundle had said, 'Could be tricky if you got caught with it, being the Head and all.'

So he was not dreaming, yesterday *had* happened.

Roddy went on into the cloakroom and hung up his jacket. He felt strangely light and new. He found himself smiling. If he could run a school, he could do anything.

He heard the hubbub of people waiting for the bell. The new Head in his office would be hearing it, too. The best of luck, Roddy thought. I gave you a good start, anyway. Then he set out along the corridor to take his place in Mrs Bigg's classroom.

Other titles published by Barrington Stoke:-

Billy the Squid by Colin Dowland   1-902260-04-X

Kick Back by Vivian French   1-902260-02-3

The Gingerbread House by Adèle Geras   1-902260-03-1

Virtual Friend by Mary Hoffman   1-902260-00-7

Wartman by Michael Morpurgo   1-902260-05-8

For further information please contact Barrington Stoke at:-
10 Belford Terrace, Edinburgh EH4 3DQ